MISSING:
One Stuffed Rabbit

by Maryann Cocca-Leffler

Albert Whitman & Company
Morton Grove, Illinois

Maryann Cocca-Leffler has illustrated over twenty books for children, many of which she has written as well. She lives in Amherst, New Hampshire, with her husband, Eric, and their two daughters.

I ♥ COCO

Library of Congress Cataloging-in-Publication Data
Cocca-Leffler, Maryann, 1958–
Missing: one stuffed rabbit / written and illustrated by
Maryann Cocca-Leffler.
p.   cm.

Summary: After losing Coco the class pet at a shopping mall, second-grader
Janine learns that the stuffed rabbit has mistakenly been given as part of
a toy distribution at a local hospital.

ISBN 0-8075-5161-9

[l. Lost and found possessions—Fiction. 2. Toys—Fiction.]   I. Title.
PZ7.C638Mi 1998   97-18203   [E]—dc21   CIP   AC
Text and illustrations copyright © 1998 by Maryann Cocca-Leffler.
Published in 1998 by Albert Whitman & Company, 6340 Oakton Street,
Morton Grove, Illinois 60053-2723. Published simultaneously in Canada by
General Publishing, Limited, Toronto. All rights reserved. No part of this
book may be reproduced or transmitted in any form or by any means,
electronic or mechanical, including photocopying, recording, or by any
information storage and retrieval system, without permission in writing
from the publisher. Printed in the United States of America.
10 9 8 7 6 5 4 3 2 1

The art is rendered in gouache and colored pencil.

This book is dedicated to my daughters, Janine and Kristin; Janine's first-grade teacher, Mrs. Robitaille; and her classmates from the Oaklandvale School, Saugus, Massachusetts (1992-1993). All the children got to take Coco home!

Kristin, thanks for the poster illustration!
♡ Mom

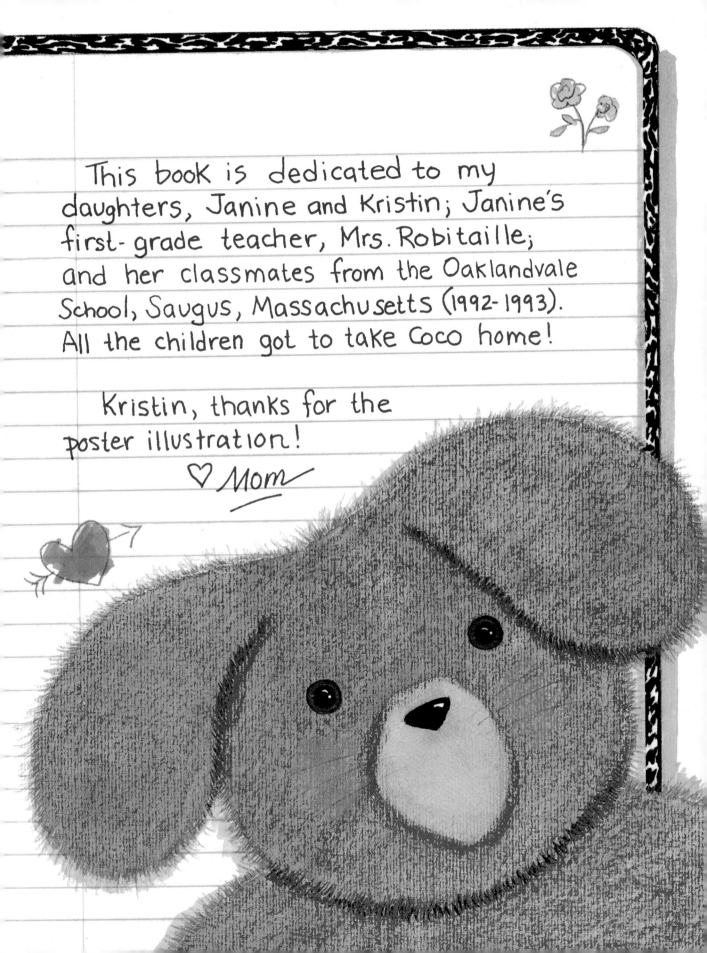

It was Friday afternoon, and everyone in the second grade was excited. Coco, the class pet, would spend the whole weekend with one of them!

The classroom grew quiet as Mrs. Robin picked a name.

"Coco will be going home with...Janine!" she called.

Janine ran up and gathered Coco and his diary in her arms.

Coco was not a real rabbit. He was a brown stuffed rabbit. He was an important part of Mrs. Robin's second-grade class.

Each day someone's name was picked from a big bowl, and that child got to take Coco home overnight.

Coco traveled everywhere with his diary. Each student helped him write his thoughts inside.

Monday:

I went home with Addie.
I met her bunny, Snowball.
He did not look like me.
Addie ~~red~~ read me Peter Rabbit.
It was a great story.

Tuesday:

I went to the playground
with Danny after school. We
played on the monkey bars.
I fell and broke my leg.
Danny fixed it.

Wednesday:
Matthew put me in his backpack. We went to soccer practice. Matthew let me wear his favorite hat. I cheered when he got a goal!

Thursday:
After school I went to the roller-skating ~~ring~~ rink with Christina. My leg is broken so I just watched. Christina's sister fed me a jelly sandwich. My fur is sticky!

Janine was beaming when her mom picked her up. "Guess what! I can keep Coco for the whole weekend!"

She slid into the car. Her baby sister, Kristin, tried to grab Coco. "Mine!" she said.

Janine quickly buckled Coco into his seat belt.

That afternoon, Janine took Coco to visit her nana.
Nana cut some carrots for him.

That night at home, Janine read Coco a story
and tucked him in bed.

On Saturday, Janine
and Coco did everything
together.

On Sunday, the family went to the mall. Coco came, too.

They went from store to store, searching for just the right shoes. Finally they each found the perfect pair, along with lots of other things.

Sale!
Sweaters

"I'm starving," said Mom. "Let's go for lunch."

They piled their bags into the booth.

"Let's get a highchair for Coco," said Janine.

"...Coco...WHERE'S COCO?"

They looked in all the bags. No Coco.

Dad looked under the table. No Coco.

"OH, NO!" cried Janine. "I LOST COCO!"

"Calm down," said Dad. "We'll just retrace our steps."

"Dad, we were in every store in this mall," moaned Janine. "We'll never find him!"

The family spent the rest of the afternoon searching the mall for Coco.

They even checked the Lost and Found Department three times.

On Monday morning, Janine had to go to school without Coco. She stood in front of the class and read from his diary:

Weekend:

I went home with Janine on Friday. On Saturday we rode her bike. On Sunday I got lost in the mall!

Please help Janine find me!

A tear rolled down Janine's cheek.

"Don't worry, Janine—we'll all help," said Mrs. Robin.
"How about if we make posters?" suggested Addie.
"Great idea." Mrs. Robin handed out paper.

On Tuesday after school, Mrs. Robin, Janine, and three classmates went to the mall. They hung up all the posters and checked the Lost and Found Department again. No Coco.

As they were leaving, Addie noticed a display. The sign read: "TOY DRIVE. New or good used toys wanted."

Addie and Janine ran to the counter.

"Where do all these toys go?" asked Janine.

"We bring them to the Children's Hospital," said the woman.

"Mrs. Robin!" called Janine. "I'll bet Coco is at the hospital!"

"Let's go!" shouted the children.

They all rushed to the hospital. As they ran inside, they saw something amazing. A big green frog was handing out toys. And poking out of the top of his basket was one stuffed rabbit—*Coco!*

Just then the frog gave Coco to a little girl.

"Thank you," said the little girl. "Look, he has a broken leg just like me!"

"Uh-oh," whispered Janine.

"Isn't he cute?" The little girl held up Coco. "I'm going to name him Cinnamon. I'm going to take care of him."

She gave Coco a big hug. "Cinnamon really needs me."

Janine looked at her friends, then at her teacher.

She cleared her throat.

"I think Coco – I mean, Cinnamon – was lucky to find you."

Janine moved closer to the little girl. "My name is Janine."

"I'm Teresa."

At that moment the frog gathered everyone together for some photos. SNAP. SNAP. He gave pictures to Janine and Teresa.

The next morning, Janine stood in front of the class and held up the picture. She read from Coco's diary.

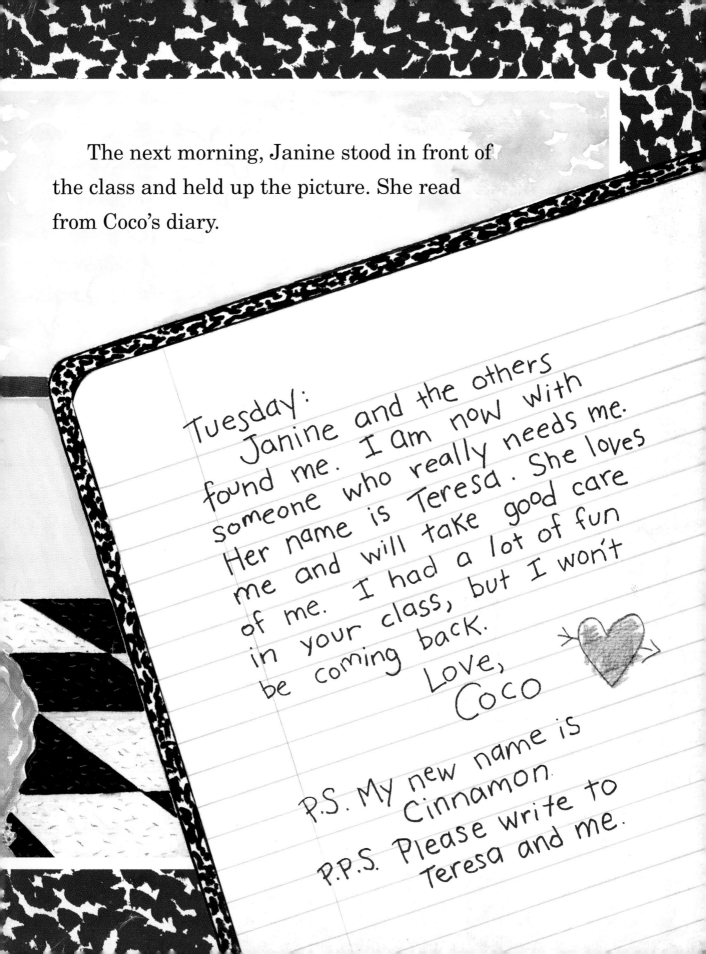

Tuesday:
    Janine and the others found me. I am now with someone who really needs me. Her name is Teresa. She loves me and will take good care of me. I had a lot of fun in your class, but I won't be coming back.
                Love,
                Coco

P.S. My new name is Cinnamon.

P.P.S. Please write to Teresa and me.

And that's just what they did.